Jane Hissey

Splash

SCRIBBLERS

OLD Bear and the other toys were having a day at the seaside.
Little Bear had never seen the sea.

'It's bigger than my biggest bath!' he cried as he chased his ball along
the beach.

RABBIT was digging a huge hole in the sand.
Only his ears were sticking out.

'What are you making?' asked Little Bear.

'It was meant to be a sand castle,' said Rabbit.

'It looks like a boat,' said Sailor. 'We could all
fit in there!'

They patted the sand into shape and
Jolly Tall found them a driftwood mast.

'THAT'S a lovely boat,' said Bramwell Brown as he brought them a towel for a sail.

'And it really moves,' said Little Bear.

'It can't really move,' said Duck. 'It's made of sand!'

'Well, it's nearer the sea than when we started!' said Little Bear.

'It's the sea that's moved,' laughed Sailor. 'The tide has come in. It goes in and out every day to wash the beach clean.'

LITTLE Bear suddenly remembered his ball.

'Oh no!' he cried. 'It's gone. The sea has taken it. I will have to get it back.'

He jumped in his bucket and, using his spade as a paddle, he floated out to sea.

'COME back!' shouted Old Bear. 'You can't go to sea in a bucket!'

THE bucket bobbed up and down in the waves and Little Bear bounced about in the bucket.

HE couldn't see his lost ball anywhere.

'Perhaps a shark has eaten it,' he thought. 'Oh no, it might eat me too!'

He tried to paddle back but he just went round and round and round.

'Old Bear was right,' groaned Little Bear. 'You can't go to sea in a bucket.'

SUDDENLY there was a big gust of wind.

The bucket wobbled and toppled and $SPLASH!$

Little Bear tumbled into the sea. His bucket slowly sank.

'Help!' cried Little Bear, as he clung to his spade. 'HELP!'

'Hold on, Little Bear!' called Sailor from the beach. 'We'll throw you a rope.'

BUT at that moment a furry face popped out of the water. It had a string of seashells round its neck and Little Bear's bucket on its head!

'I think this is yours,' it said.

'My bucket!' spluttered Little Bear. 'Thank you! But... but ... who are you? Are you a shark?'

'Not a shark,' laughed the furry creature. 'I'm a seal. My name is Splash. Now climb on my back or you might sink like your bucket.'

LITTLE Bear scrambled on to Splash's back. The other toys cheered when they saw he was safe.

'What were you doing so far from the beach?' asked the friendly seal.

'THE wind blew me out of my bucket!' explained Little Bear.

'But you can't go to sea in a BUCKET!' cried Splash.

'I know that now,' said Little Bear sadly, 'but the sea took my ball away.
I wanted to find it.'

'I know where your ball is,' said Splash.

WITH Little Bear hanging on to her necklace, Splash swam through the waves and arrived at a rocky ledge.

'Where are we?' asked Little Bear.

'You'll see,' said Splash, as she slipped through a curtain of seaweed and into a secret cave!

LITTLE Bear stared in surprise.

All around were seaside things: sandals and spades,
towels and toys, buckets, balls and boats.

'A treasure cave!' gasped Little Bear. 'There's my ball. How
did it get here?'

'I found it,' said Splash. 'The tide takes things from the beach but
I save them and bring them here.'

SPLASH bounced the ball down to Little Bear.

'Oh, thank you, Splash. But what will happen to all the other things?'

'I'll play with them for a while,' said Splash, 'then I'll take them back to the beach.'

'BUT won't you miss them when th gone?' asked Little Bear. 'Not really,' laughed Splash. 'There are always more things to be rescued. Now I must take you back to your frien

CLUTCHING his precious things, Little Bear climbed onto Splash's back.

She slipped out of the cave and swam to where the others were waiting.

'THIS is my new friend, Splash,' said Little Bear proudly.
'You saved Little Bear,' said Bramwell Brown. 'Thank you, Splash.'
'And she saved my bucket and ball!' said Little Bear.
'It's been fun,' said Splash. 'I like having a new friend to play with.'

'CAN Splash come home with us... please?'
asked Little Bear. 'I could make her a cave
under my bed.'

'It sounds fun,' said Old Bear kindly,
'but Splash already has a home;
she lives here by the sea.'

'AND who would rescue all the lost things?' laughed Splash.
'But I have something you CAN take home, Little Bear.'

SHE carefully slipped her seashell necklace over Little Bear's head.

'Remember our seaside adventure whenever you wear this,' she said kindly.

'And come back soon, won't you?'

'Thank you, Splash,' whispered Little Bear, 'I will!'

For Caroline

SALARIYA

www.salariya.com

This edition published in Great Britain in MMXV by Scribblers, a division of Book House,
an imprint of The Salariya Book Company Ltd
25 Marlborough Place,
Brighton BN1 1UB

www.scribblersbooks.com
www.janehissey.co.uk

First published in Great Britain in MMIII by Hutchinson Children's Books

ISBN-13: 978-1-908973-68-9

1 3 5 7 9 8 6 4 2

A CIP catalogue record for this book is available from the British Library.

Printed and bound in China.
Printed on paper from sustainable sources.